Simon's Surprise

To Melanie

Kids Can Press Ltd. gratefully acknowledges the
assistance of the Canada Council and the Ontario
Arts Council in the production of this book.

Canadian Cataloguing in Publication Data
Staunton, Ted, 1956-
    Simon's surprise

ISBN 0-919964-97-4 (bound) ISBN 0-921103-33-6 (pbk.)

I. Daigneault, Sylvie. II. Title.

PS8587.T38S55 1986 jC813:54 C86-093469-1
PZ7.S72Si 1986

Kids Can Press Ltd.,
585½ Bloor Street West,
Toronto, Ontario, Canada, M6G 1K5.

Book design by Michael Solomon
and Sylvie Daigneault
Printed by Everbest Printing Co., Ltd. Hong Kong

PA 88 0 9 8 7 6 5 4 3 2

Simon's Surprise

Written by Ted Staunton
Illustrated by Sylvie Daigneault

Kids Can Press, Toronto

Every Saturday Simon said to his parents, "I want to wash the car." They always said, "One of these days Simon, when you're bigger." Simon waited but he never seemed to get big enough.

Early one Saturday, he slipped outside while every-
body was still fast asleep. "Shhhhhhh," he whispered:
"It's going to be a surprise."

Simon poured soap all over the car and turned on the water. The hose hissed...and jumped.

Inside, Simon's father mumbled, "It must be raining," and he went back to sleep.

Soon there were bubbles everywhere. "Not too much," said Simon, and he put the soap out of the way. He began to scrub the car. It felt wonderful to be wet and soapy in the morning sun.

Then Simon had a problem — he couldn't reach
the roof. "Easy as pie," he said, and he went to find his
father's fishing rod.

Inside, Simon's mother pulled a pillow over her head.

Simon scrubbed the tires. He used the pot scrubber, the vegetable scrubber, the back scrubber, a scrub brush, a shoe brush, a hair brush, and his tooth brush. "Nothing to it," he said.

Still, the car didn't look very shiny. Simon had an idea. He found the polish for the fancy forks and spoons and put it on the silver parts of the car.

"I could do this with my eyes closed," he said — and he did.

Simon aimed the hose at the car. Suds and polish slid away, but now the shiny parts made the rest of the car look dull.

Simon said, "I know what to do." It took every rag in the enormous rag bag to polish the car.

When Simon finished, the car was perfect. He admired it for a long time.

Inside, the alarm clock rang.

Simon's mother looked out the window. "It snowed,"
she said. "In July?" said his father.

They rushed along the hall, down the stairs,

and through the kitchen to the side door. "It *is* snow," said Simon's father. "It's suds," said Simon's mother.

"It's Simon," they both said. "He washed the car!"

"It was easy," said Simon. "Am I big enough to paint the house yet?"